Happy Halloween, Strawberry Shortcake!

Illustrated by SI Artists

GROSSET & DUNLAP • NEW YORK
 Published by Grosset & Dunlap, a division of Penguin Young Readers Group, 345 Hudson Street, New York, NY 10014.
GROSSET & DUNLAP is a trademark of Penguin Group (USA) Inc. Published simultaneously in Canada. Printed in USA. Stickers printed in Malaysia.

ISBN 0-448-43191-2 A B C D E F G H I J

Strawberry Shortcake is having a Halloween party!
There is so much to do.
First, Strawberry needs to get some pumpkins.

Can you add some pumpkin stickers to the pumpkin patch?

Now Strawberry Shortcake needs to start decorating her house. Her little sister, Apple Dumplin', is a big help!

Use the stickers to help Strawberry decorate for the party.

It's almost time for the Halloween party! Strawberry's friends are here. They're helping her make snacks and treats for the party.

Use the stickers to add some treats to the table.

Now that the kids finished setting up,
it's time for them to change into their costumes.
It's so much fun to get dressed up for Halloween!
Strawberry Shortcake loves her ballerina costume.

USE THESE STICKERS
ON PAGES 2-3
©TCFC
USE THESE STICKERS
ON PAGES 4-5

USE THESE STICKERS ON PAGES 6-7
©TCFC
USE THESE STICKERS
ON PAGES 8-9

USE THESE STICKERS
ON PAGES 10-11
USE THESE STICKERS
ON PAGES 12-13

USE THESE STICKERS ON PAGES 14-15

USE THESE STICKERS ON PAGE 16

Use the stickers to help the kids put on their Halloween costumes.

Now it's time to play games.
Everyone is having so much fun!

Use the stickers to help Strawberry
and her friends play Halloween games.

Strawberry Shortcake is reading a spooky ghost story to her friends. But nobody is scared—they know the story is just make-believe!

Decorate the page
with some stickers.

Look! Strawberry has a surprise for her friends—
special treat bags that they can decorate!
Now everyone can take home some Halloween treats.

Use the stickers to decorate the treat bags.

It's time for Strawberry's friends to go home. Everyone had a great time at the party. Happy Halloween, Strawberry Shortcake!

Use the rest of your stickers to decorate this page.